9101 Grolier 19.00

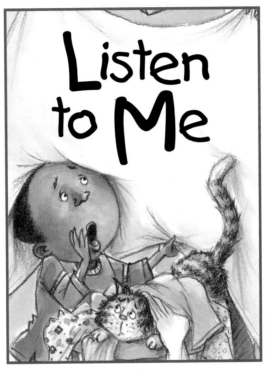

Listen to Me

Written by Barbara J. Neasi
Illustrated by Amy Wummer

Children's Press®
A Division of Scholastic Inc.
New York • Toronto • London • Auckland • Sydney
Mexico City • New Delhi • Hong Kong
Danbury, Connecticut

For my mother, Florence
—B.J.N.

To Dede, who always listened
—A.W.

Reading Consultants
Linda Cornwell
Coordinator of School Quality and Professional Improvement
(Indiana State Teachers Association)

Katharine A. Kane
Education Consultant
(Retired, San Diego County Office of Education
and San Diego State University)

Library of Congress Cataloging-in-Publication Data
Neasi, Barbara J.
    Listen to me / written by Barbara J. Neasi ; illustrated by Amy Wummer.
        p. cm. — (Rookie reader)
    Summary: When Mom and Dad are too busy to talk and to listen, a boy and his grandmother enjoy conversations and spending time together.
    ISBN 0-516-22154-X (lib. bdg.)   0-516-25970-9 (pbk.)
    [1. Grandmothers—Fiction. 2. Listening—Fiction. 3. Conversation—Fiction.
4. Afro-Americans—Fiction.] I. Wummer, Amy, ill. II. Title. III. Series.
PZ7.N295 Li 2001
[E]—dc21   00-047385

I like to ask questions.

I like to hear stories.

Sometimes Mom is too busy
to listen to me.

Sometimes Dad is too busy
to listen to me.

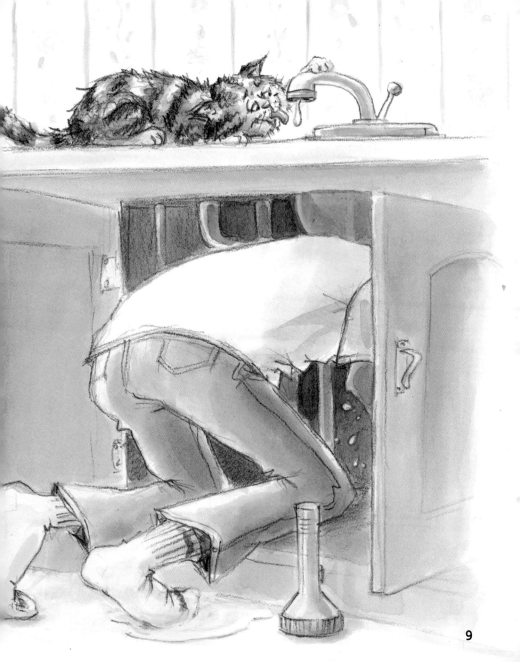

That's when I need Grandma.

When Grandma
takes me shopping,

13

she listens to me.

When I take Grandma
for a walk, I listen to her.

When Grandma drives me
to dance class, she listens to me.

When I take Grandma
to lunch, I listen to her.

When Grandma helps me
draw pictures, she listens to me.

When I help Grandma
pull weeds, I listen to her.

Sometimes Grandma and I
sit in the yard.

We talk and listen together.

Grandma says,
"Everyone needs a good listener."

31

Word List (51 words)

a	hear	Mom	takes
and	help	need	talk
ask	helps	needs	that's
busy	her	pictures	the
class	I	pull	to
Dad	in	questions	together
dance	is	says	too
draw	like	she	walk
drives	listen	shopping	we
everyone	listener	sit	weeds
for	listens	sometimes	when
good	lunch	stories	yard
Grandma	me	take	

About the Author

Barbara J. Neasi is a writer living in Moline, Illinois. She has four daughters and three grandchildren. In *Listen to Me*, Mrs. Neasi explores the wonderful relationship between a young boy and his grandmother as they listen to and share things with each other.

About the Illustrator

Amy Wummer lives and works in Reading, Pennsylvania. Her husband, Mark, is also an artist. They have three almost-grown children— Jesse, Maisie, and Adam— who usually listen.